This is little blue.

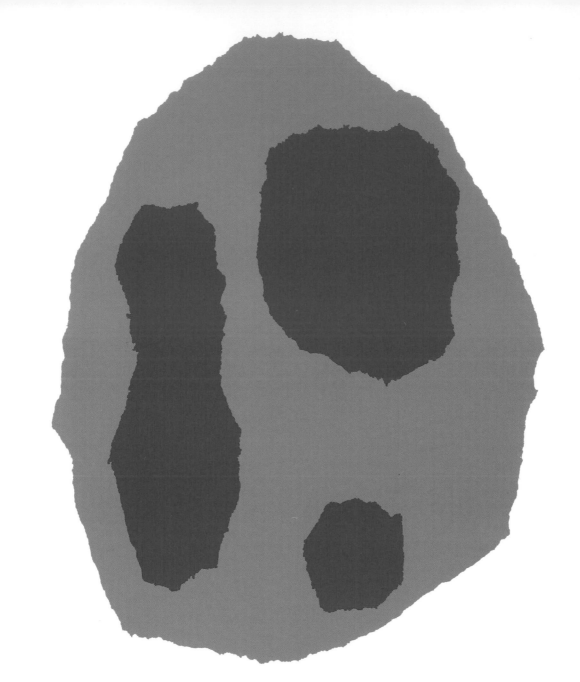

Here he is at home with papa and mama blue.

little blue and little yellow

a story for Pippo and Ann
and other children
by Leo Lionni

Alfred A. Knopf   New York

THIS IS A BORZOI BOOK PUBLISHED BY ALFRED A. KNOPF

Published by arrangement with Astor-Honor Publishing, Inc.
Originally published by McDowell, Obolensky, Inc., New York, in 1959.

Knopf, Borzoi Books, and the colophon are registered trademarks of Random House, Inc.

Visit us on the Web! www.randomhouse.com/kids

Educators and librarians, for a variety of teaching tools, visit us at www.randomhouse.com/teachers

Library of Congress Cataloging-in-Publication Data
Lionni, Leo, 1910–1999.
Little blue and little yellow : a story for Pippo and Ann and other children / by Leo Lionni.
p. cm.
Summary: A little blue spot and a little yellow spot are best friends, and when they hug each other they become green.
ISBN 978-0-375-86013-3 (trade) — ISBN 978-0-375-96013-0 (lib. bdg.)
[1. Color—Fiction. 2. Friendship—Fiction.] I. Title.
PZ7.L6634Li 2009
[E]—dc22
2008035932

The illustrations in this book were created using torn paper.

MANUFACTURED IN CHINA
October 2009
10 9 8 7 6
First Edition

Little blue has many friends

but his best friend is little yellow

who lives across the street.

How they love to play at *Hide-and-Seek*

and *Ring-a-Ring-O'Roses*!

In school they sit still in neat rows.

After school they run and jump.

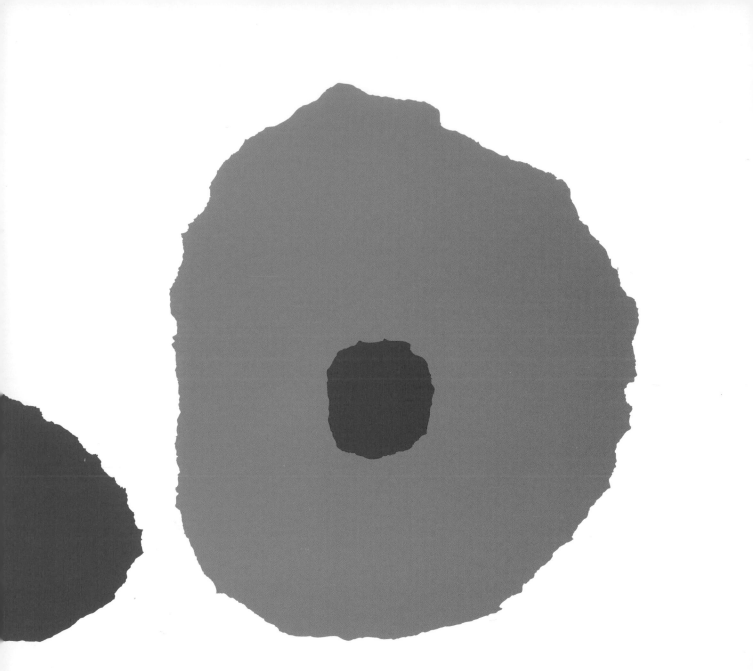

One day mama blue went shopping. "You stay at home" she said to little blue.

But little blue went out to look for little yellow.

Alas! The house across the street was empty.

He looked here

and there

and over and over and over... until suddenly we round a corner there was little yellow!

Happily they hugged each other

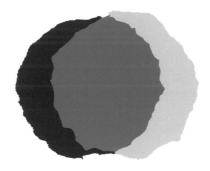

and hugged each other

until they were green.

Then they went to play in the park.

They ran through a tunnel.

They chased little orange.

They climbed a mountain.

When they were tired

they went home.

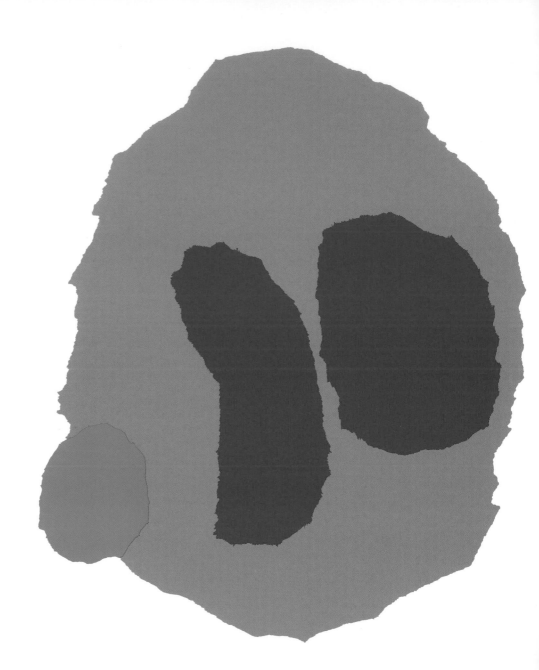

But papa and mama blue said: "You are not our little blue—you are green."

And papa and mama yellow said: "You are not our little yellow—you are green."

Little blue and little yellow were very sad. They cried big blue and yellow tears.

They cried and cried until they were *all* tears.

When they finally pulled themselves together they said: "Will they believe us now?"

Mama blue and papa blue were very happy to see their little blue.

They hugged and kissed him

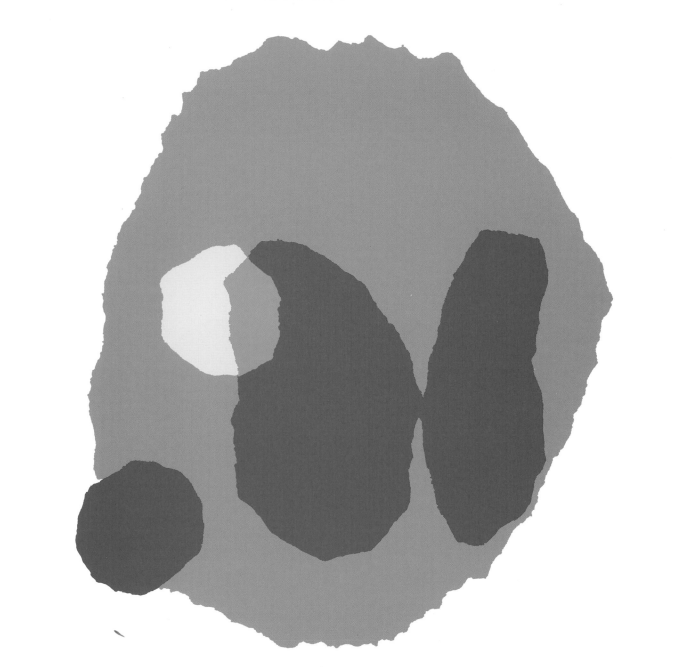

And they hugged little yellow too...but look...they became green!

Now they knew what had happened

and so they went across the street to bring the good news.

They all hugged each other with joy

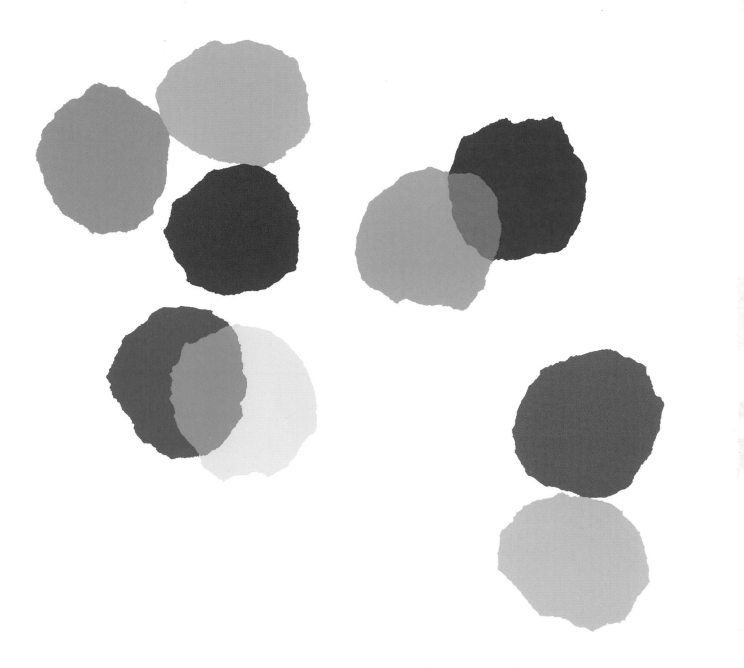

and the children played until suppertime.

The End

A NOTE TO PARENTS AND TEACHERS

Making a Book: *Little Blue and Little Yellow*

Leo Lionni tells how taking his two grandchildren, Pippo, age five, and Annie, age three, on the train from Grand Central Station in New York City to his home in Greenwich, Connecticut, resulted in his first children's book in 1959.

"They were an adorable pair, bright, lively, and totally uninhibited. It was the very first time I was alone with them, but they were intimidated enough by the surroundings and the uniqueness of the occasion to be on their best behavior.

"We were early and the car was almost empty, and in no time the two little angels had been transformed into two devilish little acrobats jumping from seat to seat. . . . Since more and more passengers were beginning to board the train, I realized that unless I did some fast creative thinking this was going to be one hell of a trip.

"I automatically opened my briefcase, took out an advance copy of Life, *and showed the children the cover, and tried to say something funny about the ads as I turned the pages, until a page with a design in blue, yellow, and green gave me an idea. 'Wait,' I said, 'I'll tell you a story.' I ripped the page out of the magazine and tore it into small pieces. The children followed the proceedings with intense expectancy. I took a piece of blue paper and carefully tore it into small disks. Then I did the same with pieces of yellow and green paper. I put my briefcase on my knees to make a table and in a deep voice said, 'This is Little Blue, and this is Little Yellow.'"*

Excerpt from *Between Worlds: The Autobiography of Leo Lionni*